BREAKING THE CURSE

BY PERDITA FINN

SCHOLASTIC INC.

New York   Toronto   London   Auckland   Sydney
Mexico City   New Delhi   Hong Kong   Buenos Aires

For Adam and Danny
(and their furry friends, Margaret and Ebot)

ISBN 0-439-74434-2

Text copyright © 2006 by Perdita Finn.

Interior illustrations copyright © 2006 by Scholastic Inc.

Cover illustration copyright © 2006 by Brandon Dorman.

12 11 10 9 8 7 6 5 4 3 2 1   6 7 8 9 10 11/0

Printed in the U.S.A.
First printing, October 2006

1 TRICK OR TREAT?

Josh was snoring in the top bunk in his bedroom. Just before dawn, he startled awake, positive he'd heard a sonic boom. He opened his eyes wide for a moment and looked around. Clothes were still scattered all over the floor. The Halloween costume he'd started to make was hanging over the chair at his desk. He pulled the covers back over his head and was asleep again in seconds.

Katie, his younger sister, was peacefully dreaming in her room until a flash of blue light awakened her. She sat up at once. Was it really the blue light again? Or just a dream? She looked around the room and listened. But she could hear only the quiet late-night sounds of the house — her clock ticking, the heater clicking on, Josh snoring. She lay back in her bed, her eyes still open, but soon she, too, was fast asleep.

Both children woke up to their mother calling them to breakfast like she did every day. "C'mon, kids, you're gonna be late if you don't get going! Breakfast's ready!"

Katie grabbed her bathrobe. Josh stumbled down the stairs in his pajamas, rubbing his eyes to get the sleep out. He came into the kitchen first. Pancakes were sizzling on the stove. His mother was standing by the table, a carton of orange juice in her hand. And sitting at the table was a naked, bald kid.

Josh rubbed his eyes harder.

Katie walked into the room and saw the boy at once. "Whoa!" was all she could say. She realized that the blue light *hadn't* been a dream.

"Josh . . . Katie," said their mother, trying to smile but looking a little desperate. "This is our newest student from the Time Flyers program . . . ah . . . Coattop, ah . . . Ketchup. Oh, dear, how do you say your name again?"

"Kahotep, O revered mother of two children who rise with the sun," he answered.

"Ka-ho-tep. Ka-ho-tep. Ka-ho-tep," repeated Mrs. Lexington, nervously. "I don't know why I'm having such trouble remembering that."

Both Katie and Josh were trying not to look at him. They realized now that he wasn't completely naked. Around his waist was a kind of half-tied white scarf. He was also wearing bracelets, necklaces, earrings, and a lot of eye makeup. Underneath all the jewelry, Katie and Josh spied his TimeFlyers hourglass. And he wasn't completely bald, either. On one side of his head hung a long, thin black braid also covered in jewelry. But where you'd really want clothes, he didn't have any. No underwear. Nope, none. He was naked. Completely. Katie was trying not to giggle. Josh was already worrying about taking him to school.

Just last month, the Lexington family had hosted Jack Bradford, an English student — from the sixteenth century. He had made Josh and Katie swear to keep his time-traveling a secret from everyone. And they had, just barely. They'd kept him out of duels and shown him how to use a bathroom, and he'd turned out to be a really good friend. But even Jack — with his dirty tights and Shakespearean swears — hadn't looked as strange as this kid. Even if you covered up Kahotep and got rid of the jewelry and makeup, there was no way he'd look like any sixth grader at Alice R. Quigley Middle School. *No way*, thought Josh.

"Your most beautiful mother has been feasting me," Kahotep said. "I have entered the kingdom of the gods."

"Oh, dear, they're just pancakes," said Mrs. Lexington, blushing. Then, accidentally looking at Kahotep, she turned an even deeper red. She added breathlessly, "Cuttip, no, no, no, ah, Tepkah, oh, dear . . . our new friend was here when I came down this morning to breakfast. I don't know why our guests always arrive at such strange times of day! I guess it has something to do with the flight schedules."

Josh and Katie exchanged a look.

"Mom," said Katie, who was always thinking ahead, "why don't you run up and get dressed for work? Josh and I'll get to know Kahotep." She gave Kahotep a big smile, and he smiled effortlessly back at her.

"Well, that's a good idea, isn't it? And Josh . . ." Mrs. Lexington leaned over to whisper to her son. "Why don't you try to get him into some of your underwear and pants? I haven't had any luck at all."

As soon as their mother was out of the room, Josh and Katie rushed over to Kahotep.

"So where are you from?" demanded Katie. "And I don't just mean what country. We need to know the century, too. We're in on the secret even if Mom and Dad aren't."

"There's a lot we've got to teach you fast so nobody else finds out!" added Josh.

"It would be a disaster if they did," said Katie. "You might not get home, and who knows what would happen to our family. . . ."

"I am from the Land of the People," said the boy simply.

Not like any people I've ever seen before, thought Josh.

"Yeah, but what people?" said Katie.

"The People of the Two Kingdoms of the Black Land. I do not know this word you use — *century*. Priest Dee-Ptah and I did not cover it in our studies when I was learning your language." Kahotep leaned back in his chair and smiled at them. He seemed awfully relaxed for somebody who had just traveled across time and space.

"*Century* means, like, what year," Katie tried to explain. "I mean, like, you know, are you from the time of knights and castles or Pilgrims or cavemen or . . ."

"Or from this planet," added Josh under his breath.

Kahotep was listening very carefully and seriously and nodding his head. After a pause, he finally answered. "Our great god, our noble king, may his glory shine each day across the heavens, has ruled our land since his father took the long journey west, twelve full rounds of the sun ago."

"What?" said Katie and Josh together.

"We're not getting anywhere," said Josh. He could hear his mother slamming drawers upstairs.

He looked at the clock. It was almost time to catch the bus. "The Black Land. High priests. Turns of the sun. I'm not taking this kid to school if we don't know who — or what — we're dealing with."

"Kahotep," said Katie, "I don't think we've got time to get you ready for this century before school. I mean, there's a lot we've got to go over before you meet other kids. All right?"

"As you wish," he said, still smiling at her. "It *has* been a most exhausting trip. Perhaps your servants could oil and bathe me this morning."

Josh just shook his head. *Oh, boy, this kid is going to be work.*

At that moment, the front door slammed shut. It was Mr. Lexington back from his morning trip to the gym. He came into the kitchen, the local newspaper in his hands, humming to himself. "Morning, kids," he said. "Hey!" he exclaimed, seeing Kahotep. "Looks like we got a new exchange student! Welcome!" He walked over to Kahotep, his hand extended — and then he stopped. "Whoa there! You might want to wrap that towel around yourself a little more tightly, son."

Kahotep clapped his hands and smiled at Katie and Josh. "Most excellent! I see your slave has arrived to massage me."

Mr. Lexington took a step backward, startled.

Slave? Katie and Josh just looked at each other, completely confused. "This is my father," said Katie, finally.

A look of absolute shame spread across Kahotep's face. He threw himself on the floor in front of Mr. Lexington, his arms stretched out, his forehead pressed to the floor. "Forgive me, noble father. Without your jewels and crowns and adornments, I mistook you for a simple household servant. I am unused to the ways of your country. I beg your forgiveness and pray that I have not brought dishonor on my family."

"Okay, okay. Get up there, son," said Mr. Lexington, embarrassed. "It's a mistake anyone could make. Honestly, I feel like a slave around here sometimes. Right, kids?"

"Yeah, Dad," said Josh, nervously. And to Katie, he whispered, "He is definitely not ready for school."

"Oh, Abner, you're back," said Mrs. Lexington, coming into the room. "I see you've met Croptop."

"Kahotep, Mom! Kahotep!" corrected Katie.

"Yes, we were . . . ah . . . just clearing up some confusions," said Mr. Lexington. "Seems Kahotep still thought we had slaves here in the U.S. of A. They must not study a lot of American history in his country. Now, what country was that, Kahotep?"

"The Black Land, noble and most forgiving father. We call it Kemet."

"Ah, the Black Land. Kemit." Mr. Lexington nodded knowledgeably. "Now, where exactly is that? My geography isn't what it used to be."

"It's far away, Dad," said Josh. "Really far away."

"Hey, Mom, Dad," said Katie. "Um, I don't think we can bring Kahotep to school with us today. We need to get him, you know, outfitted and all. . . ."

"You're absolutely right, Katie." Their mother sighed. "I hadn't even thought about it. I've got a new client showing up at the office and no time to get Q-Tip signed in this morning."

"We'll stay home with him, Mom," said Katie and Josh instantly.

"Oh, no, you don't," interrupted Mr. Lexington. "No missing school for you two. Aren't there tests today?"

Reluctantly, Katie and Josh nodded their heads.

"Well, I think I can manage a day off," said Mr. Lexington. "Kahotep here can help me run some errands. You wouldn't mind that, would you?"

Kahotep smiled widely and leaned back in his chair. "As you wish!" he answered, waving his arms elegantly. "With your pleasure, I request that we stop at your temples so I might pay homage to the local gods. I have brought appropriate offerings."

"I just hope they're not human sacrifices," whispered Josh to Katie.

Katie took a long look at the strange boy sitting at their kitchen table. "Me, too," she answered, shaking her head. "Me, too."

2 BOO!

At school, Katie and Josh worried about what was happening at home.

In Mrs. Pitney's sixth-grade class, Josh wondered where Kahotep was going to the bathroom. What if he went in one of his mother's flower vases? What if he just went in the middle of the room? There'd been no time to teach him about toilets and running water, and Jack, their last visitor, had needed some teaching. What if he was walking around town naked with his dad? What if the kids at school heard about it? He groaned out loud and Mrs. Pitney looked at him sharply. "I'd be groaning, too, young man, if I just got the

11

grade you did on your math test." *What a day,* thought Josh.

Meanwhile, in her class, Katie had managed to find an atlas on her teacher's desk.

"May I borrow this, Mrs. Chandler?" she asked during reading period.

"Certainly," answered her teacher. "I just love studying maps, don't you?"

"Yeah," said Katie. "Do you know where a place called the Black Land is?"

"You mean the Bad Lands?"

I hope not, thought Katie, but she only said, "I don't think so. The Black Land. Kemet seems to be another name for it."

"Kemet? Never heard of it," said Mrs. Chandler. And even though Katie studied the index of the atlas, she couldn't find any mention of such a place. *We've got to figure out where he's from,* she kept saying to herself all day.

Just before dismissal, Mrs. Chandler reminded the class about the annual Alice R. Quigley Middle School Halloween party. "Our class hosts it this year, remember. I'm going to need helpers to make decorations. Don't forget to get working on your costumes. We'll have lots of prizes."

When the bell finally rang, Katie and Josh both rushed to their lockers and hurried onto the bus. Everyone was talking about the upcoming Halloween party, but Josh and Katie spent the entire ride going over what they needed to tell Kahotep. "You cover bathrooms and what kids today wear, Josh," ordered Katie, checking a list she'd made in her notebook during class. "I'll go over TVs and cars and basic manners."

"I hope there haven't been any, you know, *accidents*," said Josh.

As soon as the bus dropped them off, they dashed up the driveway. Frightened about what they might find, they opened the front door, but the house was perfectly quiet. Mr. Lexington was collapsed in a chair in the living room, his eyes shut.

"Hey, kids," he said, opening his eyes and stretching when they walked in.

"Where's Kahotep?" asked Katie, looking around.

"Having a bath. A second bath, actually. That kid sure is clean."

"He's okay using it and . . . everything else in the bathroom?" asked Josh.

"No problem with that," answered their father, yawning and sitting up. "Although I have to tell you, Kahotep just doesn't know anything about America. I like these kids we get from Time Flyers, but I have to say, I don't think it's a particularly well run program, if you know what I mean. They don't come very prepared. Arriving with no luggage, no idea what's going on in this country. I think your mother needs to send the management an e-mail about it."

"What happened?" asked Katie and Josh.

"I think I need another cup of coffee," said their father, sighing.

"I knew it," said Katie when he was out of the room. "We should never have left him alone with Dad."

"But what else were we going to do?" said Josh.

Mr. Lexington came back into the room with a steaming mug and sat back down.

Katie tried again. "So, Dad? Tell us about the day."

"After I called into the office, I decided it would be fun for Kahotep and me to do some yard work together. Give us a chance to get to know each other, you know what I mean?"

Josh nodded.

"Yeah, and . . . ?" asked Katie, nervously.

"So we headed out to the mall," continued Mr. Lexington. "I needed to get a new leaf blower and I thought Kahotep might enjoy a little shopping trip . . . but I guess I was wrong. A little overwhelming for him, I think. I've heard about these foreigners who come here and just can't get over how terrific our stores are. Guess that's what it was." Mr. Lexington scratched his head.

"But what *happened*?" said Katie, getting impatient.

"Honestly, I'm not really sure," said Mr. Lexington, taking another sip of coffee. "At first, when we drove up to the home supply store, he started going on and on about how great the tombs of the kings were in Kemet. I kept trying to explain to him this wasn't a tomb, just a darn big store. But he kept rambling about how his were so much bigger and better and all that. I didn't have the heart to tell him that no one ever even heard of his country, that's how small it was. But then when we got inside, he kind of went crazy. Started yelling about holy sites and grave robbers and how we were dishonoring the dead king. He was screaming at shoppers to put back the dead king's stuff or something like that. He actually blocked the door to keep the shoppers from carrying their bags out of the store."

"The dead king?" asked Josh.

"Look, Josh. I told you. This kid has no grasp of American history. Here I was trying to explain to him that we didn't have kings but presidents and then . . ."

"What?" said both kids.

"I don't want to go into it," said their father. "We're home now."

"Did you at least get the leaf blower?" asked Katie.

"Honey, we were clearing things up with security all afternoon."

"Security?" gasped Josh and Katie together, immediately worried about what could happen if Kahotep had been questioned by any kind of police.

"It's no big deal," said their father, leaning back. "I explained he was from a different country and this was his first day here."

"What's this, Dad?" Katie had just noticed a half-eaten cookie, an apple, and what looked like a small mound of tuna fish on the mantle in front of the photograph of her grandparents.

"Oh, Kahotep. When we got back, he went around offering all the photos little bits of food to eat. Which reminds me, I ought to get dinner started before your mother gets home." Sighing, Mr. Lexington got up and went into the kitchen while Katie just stared at the tuna fish.

"This kid is really strange," Josh said to Katie.

"Yeah. . . . We've got to find out where he's from, and fast. Who knows what he'll do next."

Upstairs, Katie and Josh found Kahotep sitting on the floor of Josh's room, surrounded by tubes of moisturizer, bottles of perfume, and Mrs. Lexington's makeup case. He was wearing jeans and a sweater now, but on the top of his bald head was an enormous blob of oozing yellow cream.

"Ah, beloved sister and brother, the racing sun has brought you home from your studies. I am preparing myself for the evening's festivities with your lovely ointments."

"What's that on your head?" said Josh.

Katie looked at the glass jar in Kahotep's hand. "Seven Day Hydrating Lotion," she read.

"But why's it on your head?" Josh couldn't hide it. This kid freaked him out.

"Isn't it the best way to remain fragrant throughout the evening? My honored mother and father, may the gods bless their names, always have the servants perfume me. I would not want to appear naked of adornment before your kind and hospitable parents."

"Right," said Katie. "But we've got a different definition of naked. And boys don't wear makeup or jewelry or perfume, either. Ever." She grabbed one of Josh's dirty shirts from off the floor and used it to scrape the moisturizer off of Kahotep's head. He gave her a bewildered stare.

"The braid's gotta go, too," added Josh. "Too weird."

"No!" Kahotep leaped up and grabbed his head. "I am too young for my manhood ceremony! I will undertake it only with my father and my uncles and the high priests when I have reached the proper age."

"Okay! Okay. No need to flip out," said Josh. "I guess the braid can stay."

"Look," said Katie, pulling the atlas out of her backpack. "Let's get down to business. I want you to look at this and tell me where you're from." She opened the book to a large blue-and-green map of the world and lay it on the floor in front of Kahotep.

He knelt down and pored over it for a long time. Finally, he looked up and shook his head. "I do not know what these markings are."

"I knew it! He's an alien!" groaned Josh.

"Sshh!" said Katie. "Kahotep, can you describe to me what it looks like where you live? Maybe we'll get somewhere that way."

Kahotep paused and collected himself. He was trying to be helpful but didn't know how. "Our kingdom is at the center of the world, and the great blue river that flows from the heavens brings us our bounty. Always the sun shines and warms the earth. It is not like this barbarian land of cold."

"Wait a minute," interrupted Josh. "*We're* barbarians? At least we keep our pants on."

"C'mon, Kahotep," said Katie, standing up. "Let's go use the computer in the other room. I've got another idea."

The three kids trouped off to Mrs. Lexington's home office. They could hear Mr. Lexington downstairs, humming to himself while he banged pots and pans around. Outside, the wind was blowing the autumn leaves from the trees.

Katie got online and turned to Kahotep. "All right, Ko, let's try some names. You mentioned a king at breakfast this morning. What's his name?"

"His Majesty the king makes the Two Lands

verdant green. He is Life. He is food and his mouth is plenty."

"Yeah, but what's his name?" said Josh.

"The king, may he reign forever with Re and all the gods, is Amenhotep, the son of Thutmose, the son of Amenhotep, the son of Thutmose, the son of . . ."

"Okay, okay. I think that's enough," said Katie, typing away. "Now, I'm guessing at the spelling here, but I think . . ." She paused as the search engine revealed a long list of sites. "Yes!" She quickly clicked on a Web site, and a photograph appeared on the screen. It was an enormous gold statue of a man with eye makeup just like Kahotep's.

"Recognize this guy?" said Katie.

But Kahotep was no longer sitting beside her.

Just like this morning, he was on the floor, his arms stretched out in front of him, his forehead pressed to the carpet.

"Jackpot," said Katie.

"Jackpot," said Josh.

3 JACK-O'- LANTERNS

"Wow!" said Josh. "I can't believe you're from ancient Egypt. That is so cool! Ancient Egypt. And that guy isn't your king, he's your pharaoh." He leaped up into the air and clapped his hands. "We're gonna find out everything about mummies and pyramids and the riddle of the Sphinx. I can't believe it. This is so awesome!"

"Sssh!" whispered Kahotep, still lying on the ground. "You must not speak before the king."

"It's just a picture, Ko," said Katie.

"I can see that it is only his image," said Kahotep, irritated. "But you dishonor the power of that picture with your voices."

"Okay, okay," said Katie, and she clicked out of the site.

Kahotep glanced up to see that the picture was gone and pulled himself up into a sitting position. "Even now I see that our kings remain all-powerful. They have not vanished into the sands of eternity. Still their mighty images remain. Still they rule."

"You bet they rule!" said Josh, excitedly. "Everyone, and I mean *everyone*, is into mummies. My friend Neil Carmody is, like, an expert on them. He told me how they take out all the guts from the body and then pull the brain out of the nose with a hook and then . . ."

"What!?" exclaimed Kahotep. He looked absolutely horrified.

"You know," continued Josh. "That's what they do before they salt up the body and wrap it up in cloth and put curses on it and everything."

"No! No! No! Do not speak of these things. It is not right! The embalmer's mysteries are a secret to us!"

"Not to us!" said Josh. "You should see this

book I've got. It's got these really gross pictures in it. It is *so* cool! I'll go get it!" Josh headed for the door, but Kahotep grabbed his leg.

"No!" he begged. "It is sacrilege."

Josh looked down at him. Slowly, it dawned on him that Kahotep wasn't as interested in all of these details as he was. *Just my luck,* he thought. *I meet an ancient Egyptian and he doesn't want to talk about the coolest part of ancient Egypt.* "You're not into mummies?" He sighed.

Kahotep was still very upset but tried to speak calmly. "I will, of course, make preparations for my tomb when I reach manhood," he answered. "We must all make the journey west and be ready for our accounting with Osiris. But do I foul my heart with thoughts of death and decay? No, not I."

"Great." Josh slumped down on a chair. "So what do you do all day in Kemet, anyway?"

Kahotep smiled broadly. He was pleased to be asked. "I arise with the sun and greet my beautiful mother and my noble father. The servants bathe and anoint me. I breakfast on beer and bread. I study the words of the gods with Priest Dee-Ptah. . . ."

"Sounds like Master Dee again," said Katie to Josh, who nodded in agreement.

"Does he have a computer?" questioned Josh. "A shiny black box like my sister just used?"

"Ah, yes, he does. It is a magic device. It is how I have come to be here."

"Yup," said Katie. "Just like Jack described."

"And why are you here, anyway?" asked Josh. He was still irritated that Kahotep wouldn't talk about mummies with him.

But before Kahotep could answer, they heard a door slamming shut downstairs and their mother calling up to them, "Kids! Kids! I've got a big surprise!"

When the kids came to the top of the stairs, they saw Mrs. Lexington standing in the hallway with three enormous pumpkins at her feet. "Surprise!" she said. "I thought it would be fun for Coptop to carve them with us after dinner."

"Kahotep, Mom," corrected Katie.

"That's what I said," said Mrs. Lexington.

"Dinner's ready," called their father from the kitchen.

"What kind of offerings will you make with these giant squashes?" Kahotep asked Josh as they settled into their seats.

"Offerings?" said Josh. What was up with this kid, anyway? "These are just pumpkins. We cut faces on them and stick candles in them. 'Cause it's Halloween and that's what you do." He spooned some green beans onto his plate.

"Do you celebrate Halloween in Kemet?" asked Mrs. Lexington, politely.

"Halloween? I do not know this festival. When does it take place?"

"Last day of October," answered Katie.

"The last day of October? In the month when the fields emerge from the waters?" Kahotep had a startled expression on his face. "The day of the feast of Bastet? You celebrate the feast of Bastet? Then I will not miss it after all! Oh, this is too wonderful, beautiful mother and noble father." Kahotep clapped his hands, beaming.

Mrs. Lexington turned to her husband and whispered, "You know, now that he has clothes on, I realize he really is a nice boy after all."

After dinner, while they were laying out newspapers on the kitchen floor for the pumpkin carving, Katie had a quiet talk with Kahotep. "They're probably not the same holiday. It's just a coincidence. I wouldn't make a big deal out of it. Here," she said, handing him a marker. "You draw a really scary face on your pumpkin first."

"Why?" said Kahotep.

"'Cause you do," grumbled Josh.

"Well, actually, Josh," said his sister, "it's part of some old holiday where you made jack-o'-lanterns to scare away the spirits."

"Ah!" exclaimed Kahotep. "I thought so. It is so the dead will not leave their tombs and wander at night."

"Yeah. Sort of," said Katie. "But don't take it too seriously. It's mostly just about candy, okay?"

Mrs. Lexington was bustling around the kitchen, putting out big bowls for the pumpkin seeds and complimenting the children on their designs. "Ooh! That is so spooky, Go-Cart. What is it?"

"The Sphinx, noble mother. She will frighten away all enemies."

"Yes, I think so," Mrs. Lexington said.

"Hey, Kahotep," whispered Josh, hoping he'd get *something* out of this kid. "Do you know who built the Sphinx?"

"I?" Kahotep laughed. "The creators of the Great Sphinx are lost to the sands of time."

"You mean it's old even for you?"

"Ancient, dear brother, ancient."

"Wow!" said Katie, impressed. "I guess that's pretty old."

"Nothin'." Josh sighed. "This kid's got nothin'."

"Cup of coffee, Betsy?" asked Mr. Lexington.

"Yes, Abner," she answered. "I really need one tonight. I was showing the house on Sepulchre Street to a young couple."

"Think they'll buy it?" Mr. Lexington carefully poured a cup of coffee for his wife.

"No," she said. "I'm not sure anyone will ever buy that house. How many years have I been trying to sell it now? Honestly, I think it's cursed."

"Cursed?" Kahotep put down his carving

knife. "Is my beautiful mother contending with a curse?"

"No, no, Cupcake, dear. It's just a figure of speech."

"Because, beautiful mother, if hostile ghosts or forgotten spirits are threatening you, I would be only too happy to try and expel them."

"That's very sweet of you, of course, but I don't think . . ."

"Wait a minute," interrupted Josh. "You know magic spells?"

"Of course, pumpkin-carving brother. Is it not a part of your education?"

"Spells?" said Josh. "*Real* spells?"

"What other kind are there?"

"Hey, Mom," said Josh. "Why not let Kahotep try to deal with that haunted house? It couldn't hurt that old place, could it?"

"Well," Mrs. Lexington hesitated. "I don't know, dear. . . ."

"Now we're talking!" shouted Josh. Maybe this Egyptian kid wasn't going to be so boring after all.

4 SPOOKS 'N' SPELLS

The next morning, the kids waited in the school lobby while Mrs. Lexington signed Kahotep in with the principal. Josh and Katie had spent the whole morning convincing him to leave his jewelry at home and wash off the eye makeup. Reluctantly, he'd scrubbed his face and put his armlets and earrings and all his jewelry, except the hourglass necklace, in Josh's top bureau drawer. Still, with his bald head and long hanging braid, he stood out. Parents rushing into school with forgotten homework and musical instruments would see him, and then stop and shake their heads before heading into the main office.

Kahotep seemed not to notice their stares and

walked around looking at the artwork on the wall, the trophies in the glass case, the seasonal decorations of pumpkins and scarecrows. At one point, he stopped in front of a painting of an old white-haired lady.

Katie and Josh watched him start to bow down in front of the portrait.

"What're you doing?" whispered Josh, grabbing him.

"I am honoring your ancestors. Do you not honor your ancestors?"

"Why?" said Josh. "They're dead."

"But not their spirits!" exclaimed Kahotep. "How must they feel? I know you treasure their images. All around the house yesterday, your father showed me images of the parents of your parents and of your many cousins."

"Yeah, but this painting isn't even of a relative."

"Is she not the local goddess?"

"No," said Katie. "It's just a painting of Alice R. Quigley. She was the first principal of the school."

"I feel from her image much *Ka*!" said Kahotep.

"Whatever," said Josh. "Just don't do any more bowing. Okay?"

Mrs. Lexington emerged from the office a few moments later, and Josh breathed a sigh of relief when she announced that Kahotep had been placed in Mrs. Chandler's class with his sister — and not his grade. "Everything's in order," she said. "Kiptop is going to be with Katie."

"Mom, it's Ka-ho-tep," Katie said, enunciating each syllable.

"That's right. Katch-oo-pip. Now I've got it!"

Katie just sighed.

"Will you pick us up after school, Mom?" interrupted Josh. "So we can take Kahotep over to the house on Sepulchre Street and he can do his spells?"

Mrs. Lexington looked momentarily flustered. "Oh, yes, the spells. Well, we'll see, dear. I'll have to think about it some more. . . . Now, more importantly, does everyone have their lunch money?"

Katie and Josh shook their heads. Mrs. Lexington reached into her purse and began handing each of the children dollar bills.

"What is this papyrus?" asked Kahotep, turning his over and examining it. Then he gasped. "The Great Pyramid of Khufu and the all-seeing eye of Horus! Why have you given this to me?"

"I'm sorry, dear," said Mrs. Lexington. "I usually make lunch, but what with having to get here early and sign you in . . . well, you're all just going to have to buy today."

"*Buy*? What is this *buy*? I know not this word *buy*."

"That's right, Kahotep. Bye, Mom, bye! We're off to class," said Katie. She reached out and grabbed Kahotep, yanking him down the hall.

As soon as they had turned the corner, she explained the rules to him again. "No questions in front of grown-ups — or kids, either, for that matter. Hold the questions. Didn't we go over that last night?"

Kahotep nodded his head seriously. He looked again at the dollar bill. "But why has your mother given me this strange papyrus with the Great Pyramid on it?"

"It's money, Kahotep. American money. A dollar bill."

"Money? Dollar? Buy? I do not know these words. Please explain them to me."

Katie looked at her watch. The hall was empty and the classroom doors were closed. They were late. "I'll show you at lunchtime. It'll make sense then. Put it in your pocket for now."

Katie took a deep breath and opened the door to Mrs. Chandler's room.

All the children were at their desks. Mrs. Chandler, a bubbly young teacher with a round face, was enthusiastically writing something on the board. Hearing the door click open, she turned around.

"Oh, Katie!" she gushed. "The principal told me you were bringing a special new friend to our class today. I can't wait to learn all about him. Hello, Kahotep. I'm Mrs. Chandler. I just know we're going to be good friends." She advanced toward him with her hand extended.

Katie was checking out the kids' reactions. A

few were giggling and pointing, but Brian Bucar, the coolest kid in the fifth grade, leaned back in his chair and announced, "Radical mohawk, kid! Totally awesome!"

Kahotep acknowledged him with a nod of his head and began speaking to Mrs. Chandler. "Honored teacher who has welcomed me into your chambers, please know that I truly desire the knowledge of all that exists, of what Ptah has created and Thoth has written, of the heaven with its stars, of what the mountains disgorge and what flows from the oceans, of all the signs that the sun enlightens and all that grows on the earth."

"Oh," beamed Mrs. Chandler, at a loss for words. "Well, we're doing math this morning. I hope that counts!"

Kahotep again nodded his head and bowed slightly.

"Katie, why don't you get Kahotep some paper?"

Katie grabbed some white lined paper from the

supply closet. As she turned back, she saw that Kahotep had taken a seat near Brian and his friends.

"Hey, awesome speech, Kahotep!" Brian was saying. "Gimme five!"

"Five what?" said Kahotep.

But before Brian could answer, Katie had dropped the paper on Kahotep's desk and taken a seat beside him. Mrs. Chandler was again scribbling long-division equations across the board. Katie was copying them onto her paper when she heard a loud, banging sound. Kahotep had taken off one of his borrowed sneakers and was pounding it against his paper. Everyone was staring at him.

Kahotep looked up and noticed that Mrs. Chandler was obviously alarmed. "Forgive me, noble teacher. I had no mallet with which to beat my papyrus, so I have used this shoe."

"Oh," said Mrs. Chandler.

"The quality and color of this papyrus is truly fine," continued Kahotep. Before he could say anything else, Katie interrupted him with a whisper. "We don't do that here."

Brian gave Kahotep the thumbs-up. "Cool way to distract the teacher! Way to go, Ko!" A few of Brian's friends joined in. "Way to go, Ko! Way to go, Ko!"

Kahotep leaned back in his chair and rested his bare foot on the edge of the desk. A moment later, Katie looked over and all the boys were sitting that way.

"Ahem!" said Mrs. Chandler, politely. "Shoes stay on in this class, young man. And feet stay on the floor." She tapped his foot gently with her hand. "I'd like to see everyone get to work on these problems. Now."

As she moved around the room, answering questions and checking children's work, Kahotep put his sneaker back on. After he copied the equations, he stared at them for a long time. Eventually, Mrs. Chandler made her way to his desk and knelt beside him.

"Are you having trouble, dear?" she asked.

"I do not know these symbols of the gods," he answered.

"You don't know numbers?"

"No, noble teacher. I know numbers. I know one, two, three, but not how I should use them."

"Ah! You haven't done division in your school yet?"

Kahotep shook his head.

"Have you done multiplication?" asked Mrs. Chandler.

Kahotep looked bewildered and didn't answer. Mrs. Chandler wrote some problems on his paper and again Kahotep just shook his head.

"Oh, dear," she said. "I guess you're going to need some after-school study sessions. I'll give Katie's mom a call and let her know you'll be staying late."

"Noble teacher, I will work with you as you wish, but this afternoon I will be helping Mrs. Lexington to remove a curse from a haunted house."

The room was silent. Kids sat completely still, their pencils poised in midair, staring at the new kid and wondering what was going to happen next. Mrs. Chandler, a panicked smile frozen on her face, was thinking she had to tell the principal that it really wasn't fair to put new children in her class without any notice. Katie was trying to concoct some explanation about Halloween and a movie they'd watched last night, when Brian Bucar broke the silence.

"Spells? Haunted houses?" he said. "This kid is totally awesome!"

By lunchtime, every kid in the school had heard about what Kahotep had announced in Mrs. Chandler's class. Standing in line at the cafeteria, Katie noticed everyone whispering and pointing at him.

Katie was trying to hear what they were saying, but she was also guiding Kahotep through the lunch line. He kept picking up his milk carton and staring at it. When they reached the cash register, Katie told him to give the lady his dollar bills. He looked startled.

"She will accept two pieces of papyrus for all this food?" he whispered.

"Yes. Now give her the dollar bills Mom gave you."

Kahotep took the two dollar bills out of his

pocket, carefully unfolded them, and gave them hesitantly to the cafeteria lady.

"Thanks, sweetie," she said. "Here's your change." She handed him two quarters.

"Take them!" urged Katie when Kahotep just stood there, dumbfounded. The kids behind them were getting impatient.

"Is a picture of the Great Pyramid so valuable that I can receive food and silver for it? Or is it some rare kind of papyrus that the lady desired?"

"Well, neither really, Ko," Katie said, navigating her way through the cafeteria as she looked for a place to sit. "It's just money. You know, money."

"Over here, Ko-man!" Brian Bucar and his friends waved their hands at Kahotep and Katie, but Katie pulled Kahotep to an empty table near the playground door.

"Here. And no more talk about spells, okay?" Katie sat down with Kahotep and showed him how to open his milk carton and use a straw.

At that moment, Josh appeared, tray in hand, and slid into a seat at their table. "Hey, guys! That spell stuff is all over the school. Look, I know we probably shouldn't bring anybody else, but I told Neil Carmody he could come with us after school, okay?"

"What?" said Katie. "What?" Sometimes she couldn't believe how stupid her brother was. "How are you ever going to explain Kahotep to him?"

"Easy," said Josh. "I told him Kahotep was from this foreign country where they still believe in magic and stuff. No big deal. It doesn't have to mean he comes from back in time or anything."

Katie let out a sigh of exasperation. "You are so stupid!"

"Oh, Katie, give it a rest. It's not such a big deal, okay? Why can't we have some fun with our Time Flyer visitor?"

"Fun? *Fun?* You want to have fun? Okay, look at the 'fun' you just got us into." Katie pointed across the cafeteria to where Neil Carmody, Josh's best friend since kindergarten, was talking to Lizzie Markle — the snoopiest, snottiest, sneakiest girl in the history of Alice R. Quigley Middle School.

5 HAUNTED HOUSE

The sky was filled with gray clouds, and yellow leaves were blowing in swirls up the street. Katie shivered and looked around to make sure no one was following them. She'd finally convinced her brother not to bring Neil Carmody, and both children had decided there was no reason to tell their mother that they were doing this without her. After their snack, they'd grabbed their jackets and headed outside. "We're just going to show Kahotep the neighborhood. See you later," Katie explained.

The old house was at the end of Sepulchre Street. It sat back from the road, hidden by large, scraggly bushes and trees with thick, bare branches.

Katie and Josh had wandered through its empty rooms loads of times over the years as their mother tried to find someone to buy it. It had never seemed creepy to them before. But on this overcast autumn day, the windows looked like big black eyes.

"It actually does look kind of cursed, doesn't it?" said Josh. He shoved his hands into his pockets.

"I do not yet know if there are enemy ghosts here," answered Kahotep, calmly. "But this strange sunless weather that has taken all heat from the earth suggests the gods are hiding."

"You really want to do this?" said Katie.

"I guess so," said Josh. But he wasn't so sure anymore.

"Come, my brave brother and my courageous sister," announced Kahotep, striding forward. "We must honor our hardworking mother by succeeding in this task. We will bring great honor to her and our family."

Josh and Katie followed Kahotep up the walkway through the overgrown gardens. On a rock was a small stone statue of a sleeping cat. Josh lifted it up as he'd seen his mother do any number of times and removed the key to the house. Katie and Kahotep were already standing by the door. A gust of wind blew across the yard and rattled the old shutters on the windows.

"Here we go," said Josh, pushing open the door.

They stepped into a dark, empty room.

"Now what?" said Katie, looking around nervously.

"Silence," commanded Kahotep. He walked slowly over to the cold stone fireplace and listened. He disappeared into the kitchen and dining room and then returned. He headed upstairs.

"Isn't this the moment in the scary movie where you yell at the kids, 'Don't go in there'?" whispered Josh.

Katie nodded her head. She could feel the goose bumps rising on her skin. She almost wanted to hold onto her brother's arm. Almost.

Kahotep reappeared with a worried expression on his face. "What can you tell me about this house?" he asked.

Josh and Katie looked at each other and shrugged their shoulders. "Nothing," said Katie.

"I mean it's been empty as long as I can remember. Mom's real estate office has been trying to sell it for years."

"Are there hostile crocodiles nearby?"

"Hostile crocodiles?" said Josh. "Now you really *are* scaring me!"

"No crocs," said Katie.

"But there is an angry animal or the ghost of an angry animal. I can feel it. Search with me!"

"For what?" said Josh. "A ghost?"

"Its spirit. Its image. How else does it live here? We must send it on its journey west."

"But the house is empty!" said Katie. "There's nothing here."

Kahotep glared at her. "The world is full of unseen mysteries. Come. I remember something." Kahotep walked outside into the garden. Already it was getting dark.

"Katie, this is getting a little weird," whispered Josh.

"You're telling me," said Katie.

A moment later, Kahotep returned with the small cat statue.

"What are you going to do with that?" asked Katie. "We can't mess with anything. If Mom finds out we were here without her, we're going to get in . . ."

But Kahotep wasn't listening. He raised the statue over his head and shouted at the walls. "O, ghost! Thou hidden, thou concealed one, who dwelleth in this house. Lo! Be on your way! Flee! Beware, hidden one, be on your guard and escape!" Letting out a bloodcurdling yell, Kahotep hurled the statue at the fireplace. It shattered into a thousand pieces.

"No!" screamed Josh and Katie.

At that moment, a light flashed across the room and a dark shadow appeared in the doorway.

"Ghosts!" screamed Josh, terrified. "Help!"

"Oh, stop!" said Katie, looking over at the doorway. "It's just Neil Carmody!"

"Wow!" Neil said when he saw them. "This is better than the haunted house at the amusement park I went to last year!"

"Who's with you?" demanded Katie.

"Silence!" yelled Kahotep. "You have interrupted the spell just as the ghost was leaving."

"What ghost?" said another voice that Josh and Katie instantly recognized.

"Oh, no," said Josh.

"What did I tell you?" Katie glared at her brother.

Lizzie Markle appeared in the doorway beside Neil. "Are you guys really holding a séance? Because if you are, I'm going to tell my mother. And besides, you shouldn't be in this house without permission, should you?"

"Where'd she come from, Neil?" asked Josh.

"I had to bring her. I wasn't going to come when you told me not to, but Lizzie said we had to follow you. If we didn't, she was going to tell my mom what grade I got on my math test today. I mean, what could I do?"

"I still might tell her," said Lizzie. "If somebody doesn't tell *me* what's going on right this second."

"Nothing, Lizzie," said Katie. A hollow gust of wind blew up from nowhere and slammed the door shut.

"There!" said Kahotep, in despair. "The spirit

has reentered the room and we have failed. We cannot try again until seven suns have passed across the sky! The house will remain cursed until then."

All of the children gasped and looked around. The last late afternoon light had vanished and the room was almost completely black. Above their heads, they heard a strange scratching noise. It grew louder and louder. There was banging and rustling. They heard it on the wooden stairs. *Click, clack. Flump, flump.*

"Ah!" screamed Lizzie as a strange object hurled toward their feet. All the kids lunged for the door in an instant and spilled out onto the porch.

"It's a mummy!" yelled Josh. There at the open door, unraveling its white bandages as it rolled toward them, was a strange writhing bundle.

"Oh my gosh. It *is* a mummy!" cried Neil Carmody. He looked like he was about to pass out.

"A mummy?" questioned Katie. Looking more closely, she saw a small orange paw emerge from beneath a cardboard roll of toilet paper.

"*Mew,*" said a voice.

"Mieu!" Kahotep said, delighted. He reached down and untangled the kitten from the roll of paper. Another kitten came scampering out from the house, and another — a mother cat, holding a third kitten by the nape of its neck, followed him. "It's a mieu! And another mieu! And another!" Kahotep picked up all three kittens in his arms and buried his face in their fur.

"It's just kittens," whispered Neil Carmody to himself, trying to calm down.

"Yeah, just kittens," said Josh, catching his breath.

"I hate kittens," said Lizzie Markle, backing away.

The mother cat rubbed against Katie's legs. But just as Katie reached down to pet the cat, she noticed a shadow pass across the window inside the house.

6 FRIDAY NIGHT

"Please, Mom! Please?" said Katie, holding a small orange fluffball in her hands. "Look at his feet, Mom! Aren't they adorable? How can you say no?"

Not only were all the kittens ginger-colored, but they all had enormous feet. The mother cat, who had been settled with her little ones in a box in the kitchen, had the usual number of toes, but all her kittens were double-pawed. Sometimes when they ran too fast, they stumbled over them. It looked like they were wearing oversize baseball mitts.

"They are adorable," admitted Mrs. Lexington, weakening. "But three kittens? That's just too many. Since you found them on the road, I think we need to bring at least two of them and the mother to the shelter. That way if they belong to anyone, their owner can find them."

"What is this shelter? A special temple to Bastet, the cat goddess?" Kahotep was lying on the couch with two of the kittens curled up and purring on his chest.

"It's a place where people can adopt them — or put them to sleep if no one does," said Katie angrily.

"That won't happen to these, darling," assured her mother.

"Put them to sleep?" questioned Kahotep. "Why do mieus need to be put to sleep? They sleep all the time." He pointed at the ones on his chest.

"They kill them, Kahotep. Isn't that horrible?" said Katie.

"*Kill them?*" Kahotep pulled the kittens closer to him. "People kill kittens? Why, you *are* savages and barbarians! I cannot believe you kill the most sacred animals of all! In Kemet, such people are put to death."

"You kill people who kill cats?" asked Josh.

"Yes!" said Kahotep, fiercely. "Because they do not respect life, they deserve to die."

"Seems like a good idea to me!" said Katie.

"But the furniture . . ." Mrs. Lexington sighed helplessly, looking at her upholstered couch and already imagining what three kittens would do to it.

"Ah!" said Kahotep. "My mother has the same difficulties with our mieus, but she smears the chairs with gazelle dung and that keeps them away. I recommend it."

"Oh!" said Mrs. Lexington, who loved housekeeping tips. "I'll have to see if they carry that at the mall."

"So we can keep them, Mom?" pleaded Katie.

"I guess for now." Mrs. Lexington sighed.

Kahotep, delighted to be able to keep the kittens, was in a lively mood all through dinner. He kept the kittens in his lap and fed them bits of food from his plate. He praised Mrs. Lexington for her cooking (which made her blush) and questioned Mr. Lexington about his travels.

"Have you visited many lands, noble father?"

"Me? Oh, no." Mr. Lexington laughed. "We took the kids upstate once to see the Sasamassett Caves — remarkable things, those caves — but I'm sure you know how expensive airfares are these days."

Kahotep nodded his head wisely. "My parents, too, prefer to stay home. I am the first member of my family to travel beyond Kemet."

"And good for you," said Mrs. Lexington.

Katie and Josh listened nervously. Whenever one of their Time Flyers started talking, there was no telling what they might say. But before Kahotep let anything slip, the phone rang.

Mrs. Lexington answered it smiling, but within moments she was frowning and nodding her head. "Yes, yes, I see. But they are just children and it is almost Halloween. . . ." After that, she didn't seem able to get a word in edgewise. She would try to speak and then go back to nodding her head. She bit her lip, looked over at Kahotep, and finally hung up the phone.

"Who was that?" asked Katie.

"Just Mrs. Markle," answered Mrs. Lexington, distractedly. "Kids, why don't you go upstairs and get ready for bed?"

"What'd Lizzie's mom say?" asked Josh.

"You know Mrs. Markle, Josh. She can get a little overexcited sometimes. Remember how she claimed Lizzie was supposed to star in the school play but that you and Katie had her kidnapped? Such silliness."

Josh and Katie exchanged a look and didn't say a word. Technically, it hadn't been them, of course, but Jack, their Elizabethan Time Flyer who had "detained" Lizzie.

"But what'd she say?" badgered Katie.

"Nothing that matters," said Mrs. Lexington, firmly. "Off to bed!"

The kids headed upstairs, but after a few moments, Katie tiptoed back down to listen in on her parents.

"Oh, the poor kids!" her father was saying. "They were so looking forward to it."

Then her mother spoke again, but her voice

was low and quiet and Katie couldn't make anything else out.

Lying in her bed that night, Katie couldn't sleep. She listened to her parents cleaning up downstairs and to the hum of the furnace, and worried about Lizzie Markle. What had she done this time? One of the kittens wandered into her room and sat on the floor beside her bed, meowing. She picked it up to cuddle and before she knew it, she was asleep.

Katie woke up in the dark to realize that someone was sitting on the edge of her bed.

"Who's there?" she said.

"It is just I, peaceful sister who snores gently in the night."

"Kahotep! You scared the wits out of me!" Katie turned on the light. "What are you doing here?"

"I have had a dream."

Katie fell back on her pillow, exhausted. "Yeah? So?"

"I cannot wake up our brother who snores most loudly to tell it to him."

"What time is it, anyway?" She looked over at

the clock on her dresser. Two-thirty. The middle of the night. No wonder she could barely open her eyes.

"We must wake our brother and our parents," urged Kahotep. "This dream. It is very important."

"Kahotep. No dream is important at two-thirty in the morning. Go back to bed."

"No!" said Kahotep. Normally so calm, he looked terrified.

"All right, we'll wake Josh, but not my parents. No way. Get me a glass of water from the bathroom."

"Why do we need water? Do you use it in dream divination?"

"Nope. Just brother waking."

A few sprinkles later and Josh was spluttering awake. After he'd stopped swinging his arms around, trying to hit whomever had soaked him, Katie and Kahotep climbed up on the top bunk with him.

"Katie Lexington, I told you never to do that to me ever again!" he screamed at her when her face appeared at the top of the ladder.

"Shh, bro! Don't wake Mom and Dad. Apparently it's an emergency. Kahotep here has had a bad dream."

"Big deal," said Josh. "Grab a teddy bear and go back to bed!"

"No, my well-watered-but-no-longer-sleeping brother," said Kahotep. "We must understand this message from the unseen world. I dreamt I was wearing white sandals, don't you see?"

"True. I wouldn't want to be seen in white sandals, either, but it's not exactly the *Nightmare on Elm Street*, Ko."

"Why don't you tell us the whole dream, Kahotep?" said Katie.

"I walked near the banks of the river," began Kahotep. "Crocodiles slipped into the water all around me, and a dog with six legs appeared. It bit a crocodile and then swallowed it whole like a snake. The crocodile then became a cat with a face like the sun and grew bigger and bigger and bigger until I . . . I woke up!"

"No hostile crocs here." Josh sighed. "Remember, we told you?"

"But don't you see?" pleaded Kahotep. "The extra legs, the crocodile entering the water, and the white sandals. All of this bodes ill! Have you no dream book we can consult on the meaning of these images? We must find out what evil is lurking nearby!"

"I thought we got rid of all the evil ghosts!" said Josh.

"No. Don't you remember? The spell was interrupted and the angry spirit reentered the home. But worse than that is coming. I cannot tell if it is plagues or locusts or famine. We must find out."

"Plagues? Locusts? Famine?" said Katie. "We don't have those here, either."

"What if we go back and finish the spell? I'm awake now, anyway," said Josh.

"I have told you this, loud-snoring brother of the top bunk. We cannot try again until the seventh sun." Kahotep looked out the window at the dark night sky. "And I do not know if I will still be here then."

"You're only staying a week?" said Katie.

"Yes. My parents are visiting the Great

Pyramids, and I must be there when they return, says Priest Dee-Ptah. They must never know I have gone from home."

"Have you checked the hourglass?" asked Josh. Every kid from Time Flyers carried a special golden hourglass. Sand flowed through it in only one direction and when it ran all the way through, whoever was holding it would hurtle back through time to where they came from.

"Each day I look at the hourglass as Priest Dee-Ptah instructed me," said Kahotep. "But my dream is about something bad that will happen soon. My most noble and all-seeing mother once dreamt she was killing an ox, and the very next day my father was promoted at the temple. You see?"

Katie and Josh looked blankly at him.

Kahotep was shaking. Again, he peered out the window into the darkness. "Something bad will happen," he whispered. "I can feel it now. Some kind of evil is near."

7 WITCHES' BREW

Nothing particularly evil happened the next morning. Outside, the sky was blue and the day warm enough to leave jackets unzipped. On the bus, Brian Bucar sat behind Kahotep and wanted to talk about Halloween.

"So what are you going to be?" he asked.

"We don't know yet," said Josh, answering for Kahotep.

"I thought it would be really cool if a bunch of us were all mummies!"

"What?" said Kahotep, startled. "My time has not yet come. Speak not of it."

"Yeah! Yeah!" said Brian. "Let's keep it a secret. You could come to my house, and we could get all wrapped up before the Halloween party and then arrive and freak everyone out. Wouldn't that be great?"

"We'll see," answered Josh again. Kahotep wasn't listening but peering uneasily out the window as if he were looking for something. *Locusts, maybe,* thought Josh.

As they walked through the school lobby to their classroom, Katie noticed Mrs. Markle waiting in the office by the principal's door. She was a small, fit woman with carefully styled red hair. Her lipstick was the same color as her red suit. But when she got mad, and she was mad now, she would often start coughing. She was having a coughing fit now.

"Man, Markle, when your mother does that, she looks just like a cat coughing up a fur ball," said Brian.

"Shut up, Brian," said Lizzie. "My mother has mold allergies and you shouldn't make fun of her."

"Maybe she should go to a vet. My cat's tongue sticks out just like that."

"*Go away!*" screamed Lizzie, swinging her backpack. But Brian just laughed and weaved through the crowd away from her.

Katie noticed that Lizzie seemed surprised to see her mother. When Lizzie approached her, the two of them began quietly arguing. Lizzie kept pulling on her mother's sleeve. It looked like she was begging for something. But Katie had a feeling from the expression on Mrs. Markle's face that Lizzie wasn't going to get it — whatever it was.

When Lizzie headed down the hallway, Katie ran to catch up with her. "Lizzie, what's your mom doing here?" asked Katie.

"None of your business, Katie Lexington. Get out of my way." Lizzie's face was bright red. It looked like she was fighting back tears.

"You know, your mother called my mom last night."

Lizzie turned on her. "It's not my fault if you keep having these freaky kids come and stay with you. Where do they come from, anyway? What's the matter with them? They ruin *everything*."

Speechless, Katie watched Lizzie pull open her

locker, throw in her coat, and then slam it shut. Katie headed off to her own classroom.

All morning in Mrs. Chandler's class, Kahotep was distracted. He got startled whenever someone came to the door, and kept sneaking looks out the window. During writing workshop, Mrs. Chandler glanced at his paper and spoke to him. "Kahotep. Remember, we're supposed to be writing. Not drawing."

Katie glanced over and saw to her dismay that Kahotep's paper was covered in hieroglyphs. Brian was looking over at it, too. "Cool code, Ko! Can you teach it to me?"

But a stern look from Mrs. Chandler kept Kahotep from answering.

At lunch, Josh slid into a seat beside Katie and Kahotep. "Neil Carmody thought last night was so cool. Apparently, he woke up with a screaming nightmare about the haunted house," Josh informed them.

"We are all experiencing bad omens." Kahotep sighed. "That is what happens. We recognize the lurking evil in our dreams."

"Sorry, Ko. But I just can't get that worked up about a couple of nightmares. I mean, this is the twenty-first century, after all," said Katie, taking a bite of spaghetti.

Just then Cynthia Lubka, a seventh grader, came over to their table. "Hi, guys," she said shyly. Last month, she'd had the biggest crush ever on their first visitor from Time Flyers, Jack Bradford, and she still wasn't over it. "I see you have a new guest. Any word from Jack?"

"Nope. Sorry." Katie shook her head.

"I don't think the phone service is very good where he's from," added Josh. "I wouldn't take it personally."

"Hi, my name's Cynthia," she said to Kahotep. She sat down beside him.

Oh, no, thought Katie and Josh at the same time.

"You know, I've heard a lot about you," Cynthia said. "I heard you do spells and stuff, and Neil Carmody says you are, like, excellent at it. So, anyway, I was wondering if you could do a spell for me, maybe?"

"No. No. No," announced Katie. "No spells."

"But I've got to find some way to get Jack to call me."

Kahotep looked bewildered during all of this. He had been having trouble enough figuring out how to eat his spaghetti. "I am very sorry. I would be happy to try and help you, but, Katie . . ."

"But Katie says no," interrupted Katie. "'Bye, Cynthia. We'll let you know if we hear from Jack. Okay?"

"Okay," agreed Cynthia reluctantly, getting up and returning to her own table.

"Maybe the afternoon will be better," said Katie. "At least we're making decorations for the Halloween party in our class."

Kahotep seemed to enjoy coloring and cutting out pictures of black cats and monsters. He laughed with Brian as they made a long orange-and-black paper chain. He was particularly interested in the Scotch tape, which he kept praising as the work of clever magicians.

At one point, Mrs. Chandler sent Katie to the office to have the secretary make copies of some posters about the party. "They'll just be a minute, dear," said sweet Mrs. Muhler. Katie stood around in the lobby waiting for them. She looked at the trophies for the hundredth time and the big painting of Alice R. Quigley. And then she stopped.

The cat in the painting was an orange cat. And resting on Alice R. Quigley's arm was a giant, double-toed paw.

Strange, thought Katie. *I never noticed that before.*

"Here they are," said Mrs. Muhler, handing Katie a stack of the still-warm orange posters.

Back in Mrs. Chandler's room, Brian and Kahotep's paper chain now stretched from wall to wall. They were measuring it when Katie came in. "Ah, noble sister. Do you see our chain? It will be as long as the Great Sphinx when we are done! Brian and I want to achieve renown in your book of world records!"

All the kids crowded around Katie to take a look at the poster.

"Great drawings," said Larry Naccaratto.

"Kahotep did them," said Mrs. Chandler, smiling. "I noticed from his notebook that he is quite the artist."

"This is going to be the best Halloween party ever!" Brian beamed.

A knock on the door interrupted them. It was Mr. Walsh, the school principal. He didn't look happy.

"Mrs. Chandler, may I see you for a minute?" he asked. "In the hallway."

"Yes, certainly. Children, back to your seats."

Mrs. Chandler returned to the room a few moments later. She gave the children a long, sad look and then slowly took a seat at her desk. "It just doesn't seem fair." She sighed and shook her head.

"What's not fair?" asked Vanessa.

"Yeah, what's not fair?" added Brian.

"Oh, children, I am so, so sorry. Mr. Walsh has just informed me that he is going to cancel the Halloween party."

8 HORROR SHOW

"But you can still go trick-or-treating . . ." said Mrs. Lexington. Ever since Josh, Katie, and Kahotep had arrived home, she had been trying to calm them down. But it was no use. Every year, the kids looked forward to the Halloween party at Alice R. Quigley Middle School with its scary music and creepy games and costume parade.

"You've got to do something, Mom," demanded Josh. "Call the school. Or better yet, get the PTA on this."

"I would if I could, kids," said Mrs. Lexington. "But Mrs. Markle is the PTA president and when she gets set on something . . ."

"What does Mrs. Markle have to do with this?"

asked Katie. Ever since Mrs. Chandler's announcement, Katie had a feeling that Lizzie's mother was behind the cancellation. It would explain what she'd been doing at school — and why Lizzie was so upset.

"Well," began Mrs. Lexington, dishing out a warm apple crisp she had just made for the children, "you know how much she dislikes Halloween, anyway. Every year, she tries to get a movement going to hand out fruit and nuts to the children instead of candy."

"O nourishing mother," interrupted Kahotep, who had been deep in thought all the way home on the bus while the other kids were in an uproar about their canceled party. "This sweet food warms my heart."

"Why, thank you, dear," said Mrs. Lexington. "Anyway, apparently Lizzie has been having nightmares about haunted houses and ghosts. And so has Neil Carmody. It is Halloween, after all. But Mrs. Markle says that's the problem. Last night, she kept trying to convince me that it 'encouraged runaway imaginations' or some such nonsense.

Unfortunately, she's convinced the principal. Between you and me, I think she threatened to have the PTA stop funding school assemblies."

Kahotep looked up from his apple crisp. "Is this woman evil? Surely your high priests will not let this happen. It would be unwise to upset Bastet by ignoring her feast day. She is a wise and loving goddess — except when she is angry."

"I'm sorry, Cuptup. I know you've mentioned Bastet before, but I can't remember who she is. Is she a friend of yours?"

"Sort of, Mom," said Katie, quickly.

Later that night, when they were upstairs playing with the kittens, Katie warned Kahotep again about what he said in front of other people.

"I will be careful," promised Kahotep. "Still, I feel very concerned that this is what I've been dreaming about. Perhaps this plotting mother of the girl who disrupted our ceremony is the evil figure I saw in my dream. Or perhaps it is the angry animal spirit at the house that seeks to bring tragedy upon us."

"It sure is a tragedy that the Halloween party

has been canceled." Josh sighed. He was lying on his back on the floor, looking at the monster costume he'd begun a few weeks ago. Josh had been determined to win the prize for scariest costume this year, but now he wouldn't even be able to compete. "Boy, I hate that meddling Lizzie Markle," he said.

All over school the next day, kids were saying the same thing. In the hallways, girls clustered together at their lockers with their hands on their hips, whispering and pointing. Notes were passed back and forth in classes explaining what had happened, and by lunchtime everyone knew. Lizzie Markle and her mother were responsible for canceling the Halloween party.

"It's all *your* fault," Lizzie said to Josh when she saw him in class.

"My fault? What did I do?"

"You and that bald friend of yours. Going around scaring people with séances and exorcisms."

"Look, nobody even invited you to come. Why'd you have to make such a big deal about it, anyway? Why did you have to tell your mother about what a scaredy-pants you were at the haunted house? Why'd you have to get the party canceled?"

"I didn't!" Lizzie was furious. Her face was red and her fists clenched. "Who knew I'd start having nightmares and have to wake my mother up in the middle of the night? She hates that, you know, and she's always looking for some excuse to cancel Halloween because of all the sugar and everything. But I want that party! I was going to be a cheerleader and I know I would have won for most beautiful costume. I always do."

But no one wanted to listen to Lizzie.

Over the next couple of days, her popularity evaporated. Soon she was sitting by herself at lunch and standing against a tree at recess watching everyone else play. Katie almost felt sorry for her. Almost.

One evening, the phone rang. "It's for you, Kechoopep," said Mrs. Lexington.

"It's always for him," said Josh. "He's been here barely a week and he already knows more kids at the school than I do. I just don't get it. Maybe I should shave my head."

"That boy sure goes through my shaving cream," said Mr. Lexington, who was putting out some fresh kibble for the kittens. "Do you know he shaves his arms? Strangest thing." He bent down and scratched one of the kittens under her chin.

"He does like to be clean," agreed Mrs. Lexington. "You know, Josh, you could stand to take a shower more often."

"Mom! You want me using all your expensive moisturizers like him, too? And your perfume?"

"Well, maybe not," decided Mrs. Lexington.

"Who was that, Kahotep?" asked Katie. She had been doing her homework at the dining room table and noticed that Kahotep seemed upset when he got off the phone.

"Wise and all-knowing sister, may I talk with you upstairs about these math problems?"

"Yeah, sure," said Katie. She knew something was up. "Can Josh come, too? He's great at long division."

"So what is it?" asked Josh when the three kids were settled on the floor of Josh's room with the door shut.

"We have been given an opportunity to avoid the coming catastrophe."

"What catastrophe?" questioned Katie. "I thought the party getting canceled was the worst thing that could happen."

"Oh, no, cat-cuddling sister. While we will all be sorry not to celebrate Bastet's feast day with a proper party, imagine what will happen when the goddess realizes that we are not honoring her. Imagine what she will do to us! Imagine the plagues and the locusts and the floods. . . ."

"Yeah, yeah, yeah," said Josh. "I'm sure it will be just terrible. But right now I want to focus on the party. You think there's something we can do to get it back?"

"I do." Kahotep paused dramatically before he spoke again. "The girl who sits alone at lunch asks for our help."

"Lizzie? Lizzie Markle wants our help? Lizzie was on the phone — with you?" Josh couldn't believe it.

"She is very upset that we will not be feasting on that day."

"She's very upset no one's going to see her in her cheerleader costume," said Katie.

"But what can you do to help her, Ko?" asked Josh.

"Have you forgotten? Tomorrow is the day of the seventh sun and all will be resolved. The evil mother, the plotting daughter, the lurking ghost, the great goddess Bastet, and us — all our fates our now entwined. Tomorrow, Lizzie will join us after school at the haunted house, and together we will at last lift the terrible curse from that place."

9 SCAREDY-CATS

After school the next day, Kahotep demanded that Josh and Katie help him make an exact copy of the cat sculpture he had smashed at the house. He insisted that in order to reverse the curse, they needed to go back and do the spell correctly. Katie mixed up some homemade clay of flour, salt, and water in a bowl.

Mrs. Lexington was only too happy to provide the ingredients. "I'm so glad to see you children doing something artistic. That's the reason I signed up with Time Flyers. I knew our visitors would be a good influence on you."

Kahotep acknowledged her compliment with a bow. But he wasn't pleased with the sticky white gloop Katie had made. "We really need good red river Nile clay, but this will have to do."

Finally, they had what looked like a white blob with ears. Katie stuck it into the oven, and the kids started cleaning up the mess on the table. There was a knock on the door.

"Why, Lizzie Markle, what a nice surprise," Mrs. Lexington said as she opened the front door. "That's a lovely coat you're wearing."

"My mother bought it for me just last week. It has a real fur collar. All the other girls have fake fur collars on their coats, but my collar is made of real fox fur."

"Well, isn't that nice?" said Mrs. Lexington, trying to smile.

"Not for the fox," said Katie, appearing in the hall.

"I'm here to see Kahotep," said Lizzie, ignoring Katie. "We're spending the afternoon together."

"Oh!" exclaimed Mrs. Lexington. "I see. Well, well, well. Mr. Dee didn't send me any guidelines about dating but . . ."

"Dating?" interrupted Lizzie. "Dating that bald freak? Forget it."

"Now, Lizzie Markle, just because he comes from a different country and has different customs from ours doesn't give you any right to be rude."

"Mom, it's just a project we're all doing together," said Katie. "Right, Lizzie?"

"I don't know about all together. But, yes, it's a kind of project, Mrs. Lexington. Ew! What's that?" One of the kittens had just come into the hall and was weaving in and out of Lizzie's legs. "Does it bite?" she said, peering at it.

"Maybe you could take one home with you?" asked Mrs. Lexington, whose couch was already under attack.

"No way," said Lizzie, disgusted.

"What about a fake cat?" said Josh, coming into the hall and holding out the sculpture toward her face. Lizzie jumped backward.

"Ah, long-suffering daughter of the woman who canceled the festival! You are here!" Kahotep walked into the hall and reached for his jacket.

He may have shown up with barely a stitch of clothing, but the chilly autumn weather made him want to bundle up. In addition to his coat, he put on a hat, a scarf, and thick polar-fleece mittens.

Once they were all out in the driveway, Lizzie turned on them. "I just want you to know I'm doing this to save the Halloween party. Not because I ever, ever want to be friends with any of you."

"Gee, I thought this was a date," Josh said mockingly. "I'm heartbroken."

Lizzie snorted and walked faster.

The abandoned house on Sepulchre Street looked scarier than ever. One of the shutters had come loose and banged against an upstairs window in the wind. Kahotep stopped on the walkway.

"This time we must proceed with extreme caution. There must be no interruptions for any reason, no matter what happens. Do you hear me? None at all, or there is no telling what we will unleash." He looked especially hard at Lizzie.

"Hey, I have an idea," said Josh. "Why don't Katie and I wait outside while you two do the spell? That way, if for some reason someone might have told someone what we're up to . . ." Josh gave Lizzie a long look.

"I didn't tell anyone last time. My mother found out what was going on because I had that nightmare. Then she called Mrs. Carmody, who told her about Neil's nightmare."

"Anyway," said Josh, not listening to Lizzie. "If someone shows up, we can head them off before they interrupt everything."

"Excellent idea, noble brother," said Kahotep.

"I agree," said Katie. "Excellent idea, almost-never-noble-but-not-so-bad-right-now older brother."

"Wait a minute," said Lizzie. "You mean I've got to go into that house all by myself? With just Mohawk here?"

"That's right, Lizzie." Josh smirked. "I mean, you're the one who wants to do something about the Halloween party and all. Katie and I certainly don't care if it's canceled. *We're* not sitting alone at lunch."

Lizzie's face went absolutely white and her eyes

narrowed. But Lizzie was no chicken. If there was one thing you could say about her, it was that she was tough, really tough. "If this doesn't work, Kahotep, you're going to be in the biggest trouble ever. I promise," she said.

"It will work if there are no interruptions," repeated Kahotep.

Josh got out the front door key from under the rock he'd used to replace the statue, handed Kahotep the cat sculpture, and then sat down on the front steps with Katie. Reluctantly, Lizzie followed Kahotep into the empty house.

Fallen leaves blew across their feet, and the setting sun was hidden by dark clouds. Katie zipped up her jacket and stuffed her hands in her pockets. She couldn't tell if she was cold — or just scared. "So what do you think, Josh? You think any of this is real?"

"What? The curse and the ghosts and the nightmares?" Josh was distracted. He kept peering over his shoulder into the woods.

"Yeah. It's all just a lot of coincidences, right? There are no such things as curses and ghosts. You can explain everything. All the noises the first time were just a stray cat and her kittens. I mean, if Kahotep hadn't started messing around here in the first place, and you hadn't told Neil Carmody, and Lizzie hadn't shown up and then had a nightmare because she got so scared, well, none of this would have happened. Right? There's got to be some explanation for it all."

"Right," said Josh, but he wasn't so sure anymore. "You know what, Katie? I just noticed something." He walked across the overgrown yard toward the woods. It was dusk now and hard to see anything but shadows.

"Come back here, Joshua Lexington! Where are you going?" Now she was really scared.

"Whoa!" yelled Josh. "Look at this, Katie. Come here!"

"What? What?" Katie ran toward the woods.

"Look. Through the trees." Josh pointed.

And Katie looked. There, through the bare trees and bushes, behind a tumbled-down stone wall, were the gray shapes of gravestones. "It's a really old cemetery," she whispered.

Josh nodded. His mouth was so dry he could barely talk. "No wonder this place won't sell. It's right next to some forgotten graveyard."

"I'm getting out of here right now," said Katie. She turned around to run, but her pants were caught on brambles. As she struggled to free herself, she heard a noise and looked toward the house. A long, many-legged shadow was moving fast toward the back door. "Josh!" cried Katie.

They listened, too frightened to move. They didn't dare breathe. A door squeaked open.

"We've got to stop whatever it is from interrupting them," said Josh.

Katie nodded, grabbing her brother's hand.

"Ouch!" he yelled. "Don't dig your fingernails into me."

They tiptoed across the yard and came to the back door. It was covered in ivy and just barely ajar.

"What do we do now?" whispered Katie.

"I don't know," answered Josh. "If we go in, we could ruin everything just like last time.

Whatever's in there, well, it's in there, if you know what I mean."

Katie nodded. "I don't think it was a person, Josh."

Just then they heard squealing brakes on the driveway and a car door slamming shut. "That *is* a person!" yelled Josh. They raced to the front of the house and saw Mrs. Markle, headed up the walkway in her glossy red high heels.

"Stop!" screamed Josh.

"Stop!" screamed Katie.

"You two!" Mrs. Markle screeched upon seeing them. "I knew it. I listened in on Lizzie's phone conversation last night and I heard your strange punk friend luring her back here. What have you done this time to my darling little Elizabeth? Where is she?"

"You're right," said Katie, thinking fast. "She's meeting us here. She wanted us to help her with, with, with . . ."

"With her Halloween costume!" finished Josh.

"Ha!" answered Mrs. Markle, her eyes blazing with rage. "I finished her cheerleader outfit last night. Where is she? You must tell me right now!" Suddenly she began coughing, a terrible cough that wouldn't stop. Her tongue stuck out and her eyes bugged. *She does look like a cat coughing up a hair ball,* thought Katie.

"Mom!" yelled a voice from the front door.

Mrs. Markle looked up, coughing. At that exact moment, Katie swore she saw something small and gray and furry pop out of her mouth. But no one else, not even Josh, noticed it because Lizzie had just come outside carrying an enormous orange tomcat with giant double-toed paws. Standing behind her was Kahotep, smiling.

In almost a trance, Mrs. Markle walked up the steps and took the cat into her arms. "Tut," she whispered, holding it close. "Tut."

"What?" said Josh, looking at Katie.

"You found him," Mrs. Markle said in wonder. "How did you ever find King Tut?"

10 IT'S A WRAP!

"You're back at last! I've got such great news!" announced Mrs. Lexington, standing at the front door as all the children poured out of Mrs. Markle's car. Lizzie handed the cat to her mother, who clutched him close again.

When Mrs. Lexington noticed the cat, she sighed. "Oh, dear, not another one. I really can't manage one more cat."

Mrs. Markle looked appalled. "Don't even think of taking this cat away from me, Betsy Lexington. I've been looking for King Tut for seven years and the last thing I plan on doing is giving him up to anyone! I must come in and sit down. I'm overwhelmed."

"He is clearly a sacred being of great power," added Kahotep, patting the cat respectfully on the head.

"I'm going to get us some hot cider," decided Mrs. Lexington, leading everyone into the living room.

Mrs. Markle took a seat in the center of the couch. King Tut spread out in all his furry glory in her lap. Almost immediately, the kittens emerged from under chairs and behind plants and began climbing up onto the sofa. King Tut ignored them, but they dashed around and batted at his tail and rubbed their chins against his head.

"Well, hello, Victoria," said Mr. Lexington, coming into the room. "I see you've met our kittens."

"It seems like our kittens know her cat," said Katie.

"He's not my cat, young lady," Mrs. Markle said haughtily.

"Mummy doesn't like cats," added Lizzie, sitting primly beside her mother. "They shed."

"But, then . . . ?" questioned Josh and Katie together.

"This cat," explained Mrs. Markle, "belonged to Alice R. Quigley."

"What a coincidence!" said Mrs. Lexington, reappearing with a tray of cider and doughnuts. "I just sold her house a few minutes ago. That was my news!"

"What house?" asked Katie, sharply.

"You know," said Mrs. Lexington. "The old one on Sepulchre Street. I thought I'd never get rid of it. What's it been? Seven years now? But just tonight, that young couple I showed it to last week called me back and made an offer. They decided they wanted a fixer-upper after all."

"It sure is going to take a lot of work," said Mr. Lexington.

"The curse!" exclaimed Josh. "It really has been broken."

"Yes, of course," said Kahotep, stretching out on the carpet to relax. "I told you it would be if I wasn't interrupted."

"The haunted house belonged to Alice R. Quigley, the principal our school is named after?"

asked Katie. There was still a lot she didn't understand.

"Yes," said Mrs. Lexington. "When her plane disappeared over the Atlantic Ocean, her family put the house on the market. She didn't have any children of her own who wanted it."

At this, Mrs. Markle burst unexpectedly into tears. Mr. and Mrs. Lexington didn't know what to do. Mr. Lexington kept holding out a handkerchief, which she waved away, and Mrs. Lexington tried to offer a cup of herbal tea but couldn't make herself heard over the sobs. Finally, it was Lizzie who managed to calm her down.

"Mom, you're making a fool of yourself. And in front of the Lexingtons, too. I'll never live this down. Calm down, okay? What's Alice R. Quigley got to do with you?"

Mrs. Markle looked at her daughter through her tears. "Everything," she answered. "Everything. I was her favorite. Hall monitor. Student council president. Star of the school play. I was just like you, my precious."

"Two of them. How awful," said Katie under her breath.

But her mother heard her and whispered, "Yes. Her mother was absolutely unbearable when we were in school together."

"And when I grew up and had little Lizzie," continued Mrs. Markle, "I remained close to Alice R. Quigley. We became friends. And once she said to me, 'Vicki, if anything ever happens to me, be sure to take care of Tuttles.' I promised her I would. How was I to know that just a few weeks later, her plane would vanish? I never really thought I'd have to adopt this enormous animal. I thought he'd be all right on his own. He'd hunt in the woods. He'd survive. But my promise haunted me, and one day a month or so after Alice R. Quigley had disappeared, I went to the house with a can of cat food. 'Here, kitty, kitty,' I called. But nothing. King Tut was gone. Disappeared. I was sure he was dead. For a year or more, I looked for him, but he wasn't there. Until, magically, tonight." King Tut reached over one of his enormous double-toed paws and touched Mrs. Markle on the cheek.

"So," said Katie. "You were supposed to take care of Alice R. Quigley's cat and you didn't."

Mrs. Markle nodded through her tears and clutched King Tut tighter.

Lizzie turned to her mother. "So, Mom, what do I get for finding this cat for you?"

"Anything, darling, anything."

Josh, Katie, and Kahotep all held their breath.

"That's easy," said Lizzie. "I want the Halloween party back for tomorrow night."

The next hour was filled with frantic phone calls to the principal, teachers, and parents. Decorations had to be finished and refreshments prepared. Lizzie and her mother left to meet with the party committee at their house. They took King Tut, who didn't seem to be making Mrs. Markle cough, and one of the kittens.

Mrs. Lexington was a little disappointed that she couldn't convince the Markles to take them all, but happy that the children were excited about Halloween again.

"Let me know, kids, if you need any help with your costumes," offered Mr. Lexington, while he patted one of the kittens. He was happy they were going to stay.

"I'm all set, Dad. I'm going to be Cleopatra, and Kahotep is going to show me how to do Egyptian eye makeup," said Katie.

"And I'm going to be the ancient Egyptian god Anubis. He's got the head of a jackal and he's the god of mummification," said Josh. "It's going to be the most original scary monster costume ever. Kahotep gave me the idea."

"I'm noticing an Egyptian theme here," said Mr. Lexington. "You going to be some kind of Egyptian, too, Kahotep?"

"No. I am from Kemet."

"Right," said Mr. Lexington. "I keep forgetting. Now where is that again?"

Later, upstairs in Josh's room, Josh and Katie asked Kahotep what he wanted to be. "Werewolves are cool," said Josh. "And it's always easy to do a hobo costume or be an alien."

"Or you could even go as a superhero. Josh has some old costumes that would fit you perfectly," said Katie.

But Kahotep didn't say anything. He just looked down at the kitten he had brought upstairs with him. Finally, he spoke. "My heart is filled with gladness that I have been able to remove this terrible curse of the unselling house. And I am glad that you are excited about your party of costumes and candy. But I have come to realize that you and your people do not really understand how to honor the great goddess Bastet. A small party for children that will last a few hours? Why, our feasts for Bastet go on for days. Thousands upon thousands come to her temple to dance and feast."

"But Halloween is fun," said Josh. "We get so much candy, you won't even believe it. Really good candy, too. I love the mini chocolate bars."

Kahotep gave him a halfhearted smile. "It sounds very lovely, noble brother, but the feast of Bastet, the cat goddess, is about more than honeyed sweets."

"You sound a little homesick," said Katie.

"I must confess that I miss Kemet, noble sister. You and your gracious parents have been most hospitable and generous, but I never wanted to leave civilization. Priest Dee-Ptah felt, however, that I could do good work here in the barbarian lands. And now I know that I have. I have put things right between the cat-coughing lady and King Tut. All is at last well. But, oh, to miss the feast of Bastet. That is too terrible."

"I'm sorry, Ko," said Josh. "I wish there was something we could do for you. I wish we could help you get home. Check your hourglass. How much more time do you have, anyway?"

Kahotep pulled the hourglass necklace from under his shirt.

"Wow," said Katie. "It doesn't look like there's much more to go at all." Only a few grains of golden sand were left to fall.

"You are right," said Kahotep, surprised. "Why, the sands have started to flow much faster all of a sudden. Priest Dee-Ptah in his infinite wisdom has seen to my return. May all the gods and the kings of the past bless him."

"I can't believe you're going," said Josh.

"Me, neither," said Katie. "It feels like you just got here."

"I have only moments, beloved brother and sister, and so much I had planned to say to you. But you must know that always I will think of you. What feasting we will have when you come to visit me in Kemet."

"We get to go to ancient Egypt?" said Katie, her eyes wide.

"Perhaps, sister of the future day. Perhaps."

"So I'll get to see a mummy?" asked Josh.

"I hope not!" said Kahotep. "But I will show you the golden sands of the desert and the beautiful blue waters of the Nile. We will feast on my father's barge and race each other in chariots. It will be good for you to see what a civilized country is like. And now," he added, taking a last look at his hourglass. "Good-bye, Katie and Josh. Good-bye."

Afterward, Katie said she'd been blinded by a flash of blue light, and Josh said he'd had to cover his head because the sonic boom was so loud. But when they looked up, Kahotep was gone. Completely gone. And the ginger kitten that had been in his lap? She was gone, too.

EPILOGUE: STRANGE BUT TRUE

The school Halloween party was the best one ever. All the kids said so. In an upset victory, Katie won the prize for prettiest costume with her Cleopatra outfit. All the judges commented on how amazing her eye makeup was. And Josh won for scariest. Lizzie won, of course, for overall best, a new category added at the last moment by her mother's friends, who were always the judges. Brian Bucar nearly won an award for strangest costume. He had shown up with his head completely shaved except for a small square of hair that spiked upward.

"What are you, anyway?" kids kept asking him.

"I'm Kahotep! Can't you tell?"

But no one could.

Mrs. Lexington had been startled to find Kahotep gone when she woke up. "I wish our guests wouldn't leave so suddenly," she complained. "But I'm glad Kahotep took a kitten. I only hope he doesn't have trouble with customs at the airport."

"Mom, you said his name right," said Katie, surprised.

"Of course I did, sweetheart. It's not like it's a hard name to say."

At one point during the party, Katie stepped out into the lobby to get a breath of fresh air and a sip of water. The water fountain was right by the painting of Alice R. Quigley, and Katie took a long look at it again. Yup, that was King Tut in her arms all right, in all his orange, double-toed splendor. Katie was just about to walk back into the party when she noticed something else about the old white-haired lady in the painting.

"There you are," said Josh, coming into the lobby. "We're just about to start doing the mummy wrap game."

"You're never going to believe this, Josh."

"What?"

"Look," said Katie. And she pointed to the necklace Alice R. Quigley was wearing. It was a tiny hourglass filled with golden sand.

BACK WITH KAHOTEP IN THE EIGHTEENTH DYNASTY (1390 B.C.)

The sun is shining. The sun is almost always shining. From your seat on an elegant chair in your father's garden, you can watch the blue waters of the Nile flow by. You know that soon they will flood the banks of the river, and when the waters recede, the farmers will plant their crops in the rich soil made black from the river silt. The red deserts that surround your country on three sides protect you from enemies. It has been this way for thousands of years. You are blessed to live in a magnificent, stable, and peaceful land.

In the future, looking at your kings' magnificent pyramids and perfectly preserved mummies, some will imagine that you were a people obsessed with death.

They will be wrong. You are "The People." You know how to savor and enjoy life — to cherish your family and honor the gods. When you die, you want most of all for nothing to change. That is why your kings fill their tombs with food and chariots and furniture — so they will have everything they need to keep on living just as they always have.

"Ah, this is the life!"

Kemet

You don't think of yourself as an Egyptian, and your people won't for thousands of years. Egypt is what the Greeks will eventually call your country. But for now, you are the people of Kemet, the Black Land of dark, fertile soil.

You think of your country as being "Two Lands": the Upper Kingdom, where the great Nile begins to gather force, and the Lower Kingdom, where it spills out into the deltas of the Mediterranean Sea. Your king even wears a double crown to show that he is lord of both lands.

Keeping Track of Time

Your civilization is already over two thousand years old and during that time it has barely changed at all. It will last for another one thousand years beyond you. Imagine three thousand years. Imagine going backward from the time of Josh and Katie, back to the time of the Pilgrims, back to the knights and their castles, back to Caesar and the Roman Empire, back even further to the days of Moses. Now imagine that in all that time, nothing in your country has changed — the art is the same, the writing is the same, the religion is the same, the clothes are the same, the customs are the same. If you can imagine that, you know what it is like to live in Kemet.

Already, in the Eighteenth Dynasty in the reign of Amenhotep, the pyramids are ancient — over a thousand years old. The Great Sphinx has been nearly buried in the sands of time. It has only recently been dug out and restored.

You worship the god Re, the sun god, who each day drives his chariot across the sky. You have followed his progress so carefully that you have even created the first calendar to divide the year into twelve months and 365 days. You measure the immense passage of time by the reigns of your kings.

Washing Up

You live in a hot, dry, sandy land and you love to bathe — sometimes even four times a day. You love to cover yourself in special moisturizers and oils. Once, the workers on one of the king's construction projects even went on strike over how little ointment the workers were receiving.

You love your clothes to be clean, too, and you

even shave your entire body with a razor to keep away lice. At parties, you like to put a cone of pomade (perfumed wax) on the top of your head. As it melts, it covers you in a pleasing odor all evening long.

If you come from a wealthy family, you have a bathing room lined with stone and a separate lavatory, with a special seat made of brick. You are a very civilized people!

"Get in there now! You've only had two baths today!"

Clothing

In a hot, dry climate there is little need of clothing. At home, your father wears nothing but a pleated kilt made of linen and walks around barefoot. Your mother has a simple, sleeveless sheath, which might cover her upper body, or not. You and your brothers and sisters probably don't bother to wear anything at all! And nobody is embarrassed.

But you *love* jewelry — strings of beads made of lapis lazuli, gold armlets, and jeweled bracelets and earrings. You use cosmetics as well, to make your eyes stand out like a cat's with black paint. You use powdered malachite to make your eyelids green, red ocher mixed with grease to make your lips shine, and the juice of the henna plant to tint your fingernails.

Sometimes your parents shave their heads and wear elaborate wigs when they go out of the house. If you are a boy, you shave your head as well, all except for a long, uncut lock that you keep braided and covered in jewels. Cutting it is probably an elaborate ceremony that symbolizes your passage into adulthood.

Spending Money

You don't spend money. You don't even know what it is. Money won't be invented until the seventh century B.C. To get what you need, you barter, or trade, for it.

School

You learn two different kinds of writing —hieroglyphs, the famous picture writing, and hieratic script, which is like cursive hieroglyphs. Most of the time you copy essays and wise sayings to learn all the words you need to know. Your teacher is probably a priest or a scribe, and he believes that the best way to teach you is to beat you. "A boy's ears are on his backside," he says. If you know how to write, you are probably a boy. Most girls aren't taught how to write.

Your people invented paper. The papyrus plant grows everywhere in your country. You take the lower part of the stem, cut it into strips, and place the strips on cloth or wood. You cross these with other strips going in the opposite direction. Then you pound it with a mallet and scrape it smooth with a stone.

Reading and writing are your main subjects, but you do learn some simple arithmetic — addition and subtraction. You don't, however, really know how to do multiplication and division or fractions. But that doesn't stop you — you still accomplish some of the greatest feats of engineering and architecture civilization has ever seen.

What You Believe

Your world is controlled by the unseen forces of your many gods. If you are sick or your crops fail or an eclipse blackens the sun, it is because you have made one of them angry. But the gods can also protect you, and so you wear amulets that represent the eye of Horus or the cat's eye of Bastet.

You believe it is important to care for the spirits of your ancestors. In your home, you keep small statues or images of them and you visit their tombs and offer them prayers and food. You don't want them to become unhappy and cause you illness or bad luck.

If you suspect a spirit is angry with you, you can make a figurine of the ghost and then smash it. All the while, you are saying important incantations. If you mess up any of those spells, forget it. You're stuck with the angry spirit.

Your doctors know how to set bones and prescribe medicines. Swallowing a skinned mouse is considered an excellent way to cure sick children.

Most importantly, the doctor can determine the appropriate spells and prayers that need to be said for you.

The spirit world often speaks to you in your dreams, and the scribes have many books for helping you determine what they mean. If you see a cat, you know you will have a good harvest. If you see yourself wearing white sandals, it means you will be traveling soon.

Some of Your Gods and Goddesses

Amon — the god of the wind and air

Anubis — the jackal-headed god of cemeteries and embalming

Bastet — the cat goddess

Horus — the god of the sky. He often has a hawk's head.

Isis — the devoted wife of Osiris, and the mother

of Horus. She is often seen in sculptures
holding Horus.

Maat — the goddess of truth

Osiris — the god and judge of the dead

Ptah — the god of artists and craftspeople

Re — the great sun god

Sobek — the crocodile god

Thoth — the divine scribe and the inventor of
numbers

The Sacred Cat

Your people are farmers and in your father's houses
are great stores of grain. Who protects your food from
hungry mice? Your mieu, that's who! You call cats
mieus. Guess why? You tamed the wild cats, mostly
brindled tabbies, and brought them into your homes
as beloved pets. Cats are sacred to you, and the
deliberate killing of a cat is a crime punishable by
death. If one of your cats dies, you might take it to the
temple at Bubastis to be embalmed and buried in a
sacred urn in honor of Bastet, the cat goddess.

Bastet is the daughter of Re and the wife of Ptah.
She protects women, children, and cats, of course. She

is the guardian of music, dance, pleasure, and family. She has the head of a cat.

Each year on October 31, you celebrate the festival of Bastet. You crowd onto boats with your family. Some people are clicking castanets and others are playing pipes. Everyone is singing. Whenever you pass a town, you dance and sing and make a ruckus. When you finally arrive at the temple at Bubastis, you drink wine, have a feast, and make appropriate offerings. Sometimes over 700,000 people show up to celebrate. It's a *very* big party.

"Those were the days!"

ABOUT THE AUTHOR

Perdita Finn lives in the Catskill Mountains with her husband, two children, an overweight dachshund, and four demanding cats.
(This is their favorite book so far.)